THE BOOK OF MORMON

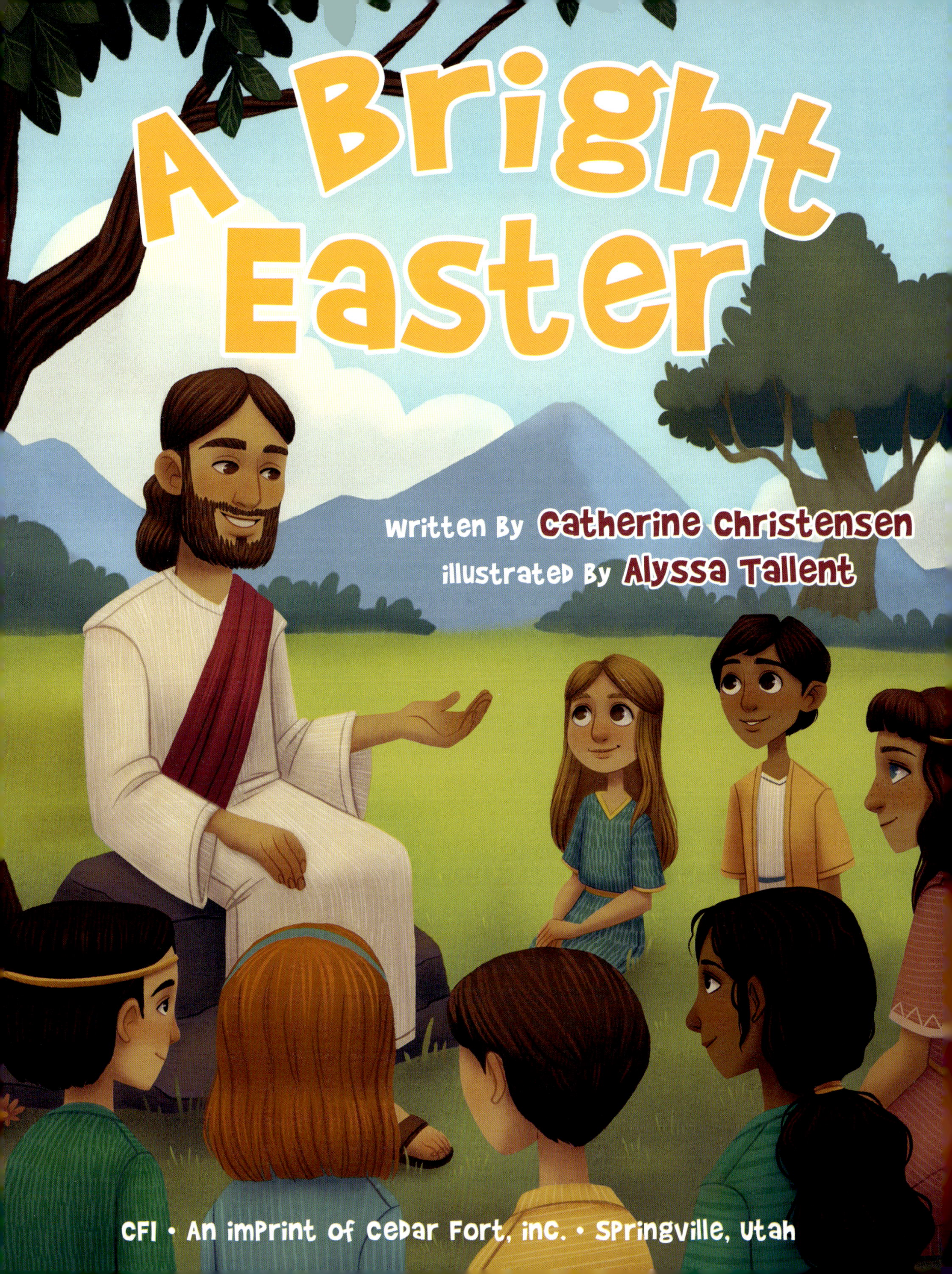

A Bright Easter

Written By Catherine Christensen

illustrated By Alyssa Tallent

CFI • An imprint of Cedar Fort, Inc. • Springville, Utah

At Easter we celebrate Christ living again.

Shine a light through the pages to discover secret pictures and activities. Learn the story of Easter and how we remember Christ now.

Bonus Easter Egg Hunt: On every page, search for a hidden Easter Egg.

We remember Jesus's final week in different ways all around the world. What fun Easter traditions can you find?

- Corfu, Greece: Throw pots out of windows
- Bermuda: Fly kites
- Germany: Decorate trees with Easter eggs
- England: Roll eggs down a hill
- USA: Hunt for Easter eggs

When Jesus rode into Jerusalem, people shouted "Hosanna" in excitement and waved palm branches.
What did Jesus ride on?
What other animals can you spot?

Hosanna means “Please save us” in Hebrew. The crowds believed Jesus was their Savior.

Easter arrives with springtime. The world comes alive again with new flowers and baby animals. Can you find ten newly hatched chicks?

All the new life at Easter time reminds us that Christ lived again after death.

During Christ's final week, children gathered around Jesus at the temple to hear Him teach. He also healed those who were sick and injured.

Can you find the hidden pictures of modern temples?

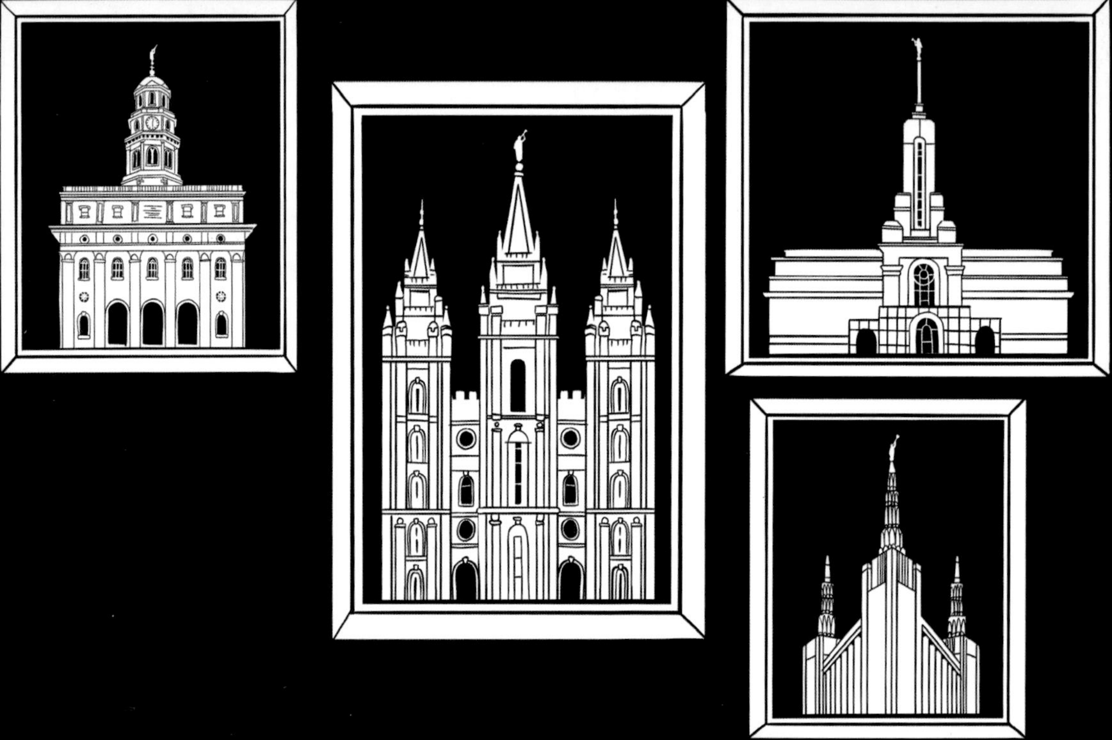

Christ kept the temple in Jerusalem a sacred place. We can show reverence to our temples now too.

We can serve others as Jesus did. How could you help in each of these photos?

When we help other people,
we become more like Jesus.

Jesus climbed the Mount of Olives to teach. Find the path through the olive trees to join those who listened to His words.

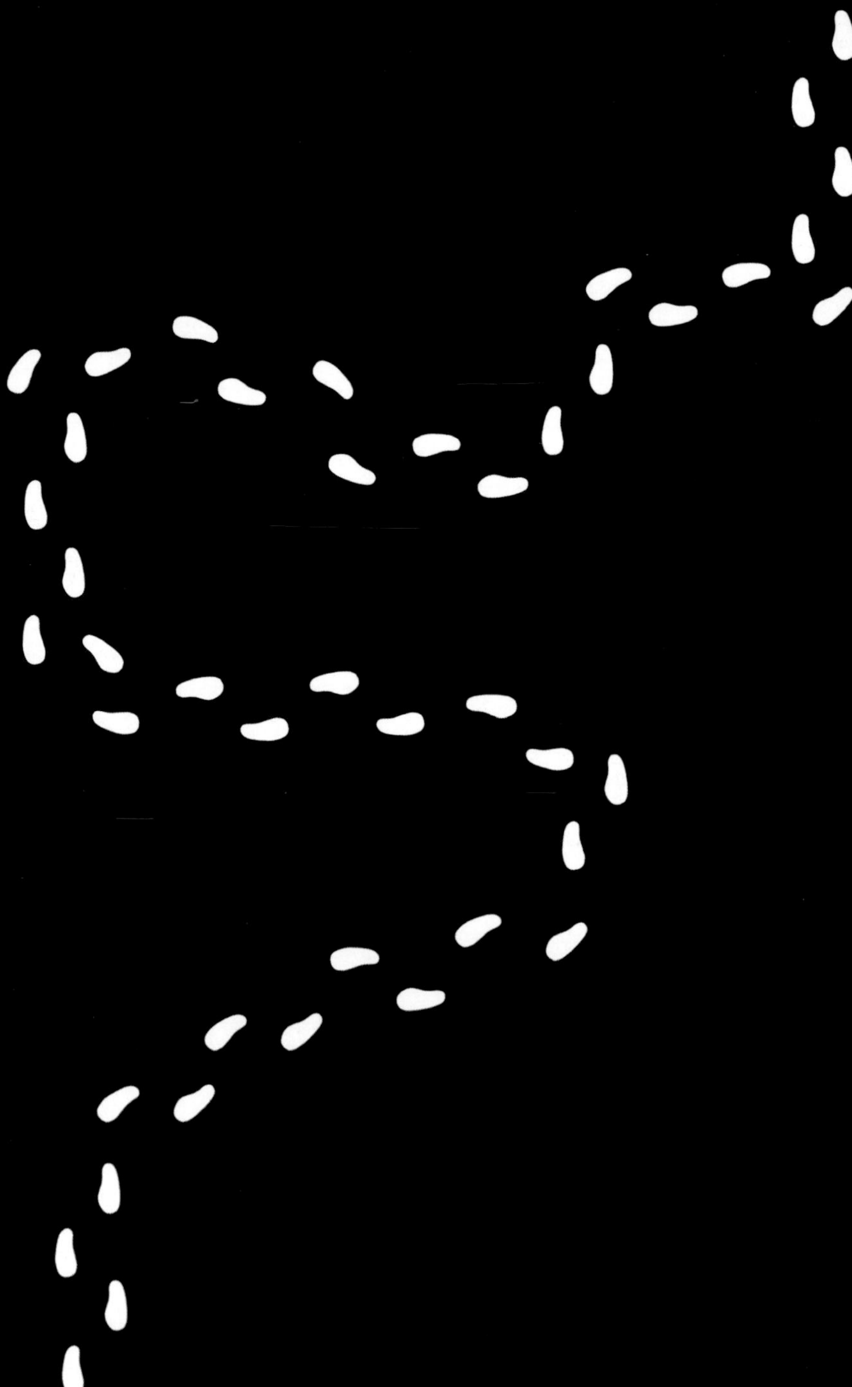

Jesus taught the people in parables—stories that helped them learn.

We can still listen to Jesus's words today through the scriptures and prophets. Can you figure out the missing words of this scripture? Which story is this boy reading about?

Jesus visited the Nephite children after He was resurrected. Children in the Old World and the New World were part of the Easter story.

Jesus and His twelve Disciples gathered in an upper room for the Last Supper. They shared bread and wine to remember the sacrifice He was about to make.

Can you spot which items around the room shouldn't be there?

We still take bread and water every Sunday to remember Jesus. This is a special time to think of Him.

Which of the children in church are thinking of Jesus?

The sacrament helps us remember the Easter story all year long.

Jesus found a quiet, peaceful garden called Gethsemane where He could kneel and pray. He atoned for all our mistakes and hurts. Who was with Jesus through this sacred experience?

An angel comforted
and supported Jesus.

Christ's Atonement Can Bless Us. What Symbols of the Atonement's Blessings Can You Find?

- Dove = Peace
- Heart = Hope and love
- Water Drops = Becoming clean
- Band-Aid = Healing
- The open tomb = Living again

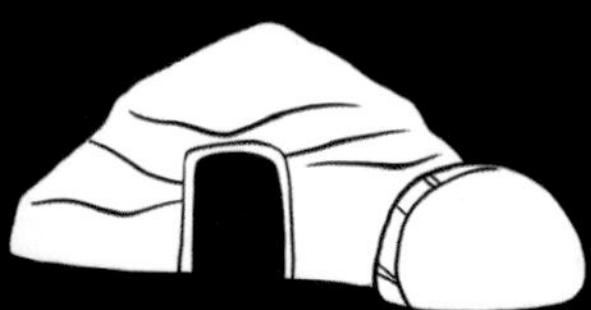

Jesus died on the cross and was laid in a tomb. When Mary visited, the huge stone was rolled away. Who did Mary see at the tomb?

The resurrected Christ. Jesus lived again. He overcame death so that we can all live with Him again one day.

Because of what Jesus did, we can live again with our families forever. Which member of her family does this girl most look like?

Our eternal families include our ancestors who love and help us. We can be with them and Jesus forever, all because of what happened that first Easter.

Fun Easter traditions can remind us what Jesus did for us. Easter eggs represent the tomb rolling open revealing the living Christ. Can you help these children find all the Easter eggs?

The meaning behind our Easter traditions can help us focus on the Savior.

On that first Easter, Christ gave us hope and light. Easter is a time to celebrate and share Christ's light with others. Jesus is the Light of the World. How can you be a light this Bright Easter?

To my friends at Cedar Fort, old and new, for sticking with me through all these books. And to the bright lights in my life: my wonderfully supportive family.
—Catherine

To Evan. Thanks for being the sweetest toddler I could ask for and for taking long naps while I worked on this book.
—Alyssa

ISBN 13: 978-1-4621-2298-1

Published by CFI, an imprint of Cedar Fort, Inc.
2373 W. 700 S., Springville, UT 84663
Distributed by Cedar Fort, Inc., www.cedarfort.com

Library of Congress Control Number: 2018962224

Cover design and typesetting by Shawnda T. Craig

Edited by Kaitlin Barwick

Printed in the United States of America

10 9 8 7 6 5 4 3 2 1

Printed on acid-free paper

THE BOOK OF MORMON